I SPY with
INSPECTOR STILTON

Judith Rossell

LITTLE HARE

Inspector Stilton and his young assistant, Nat, were in their office when the phone rang. It was Professor Pyramid, the curator of the town museum.

"Twelve of our most precious treasures have been stolen from the Egyptian collection!' he cried. "Please come at once!"

"We'll be right there," the detective promised. He hung up the phone and turned to his assistant. "We've got a case to solve, Nat—let's go see Professor Pyramid."

"I can already see five pyramids right here in this room," Nat replied.

At the museum, Professor Pyramid showed the detectives photos of the stolen objects.

"A witness saw the thief run out of the museum with a big bag and disappear down a street of shops," the curator explained. "The empty bag was found at the end of the street—but there was no sign of the treasure."

Inspector Stilton and Nat stepped out onto the street.

"Very curious," said the inspector. "I've already seen one of the missing pieces—the blue scarab. The thief must have hidden it, and is planning to come back for it later. My guess is we will find all the stolen objects along this street. Let's start by interviewing the shopkeepers."

"I can't see the hidden scarab," said Nat, "but I can see ten hidden stars."

Mrs Floss, Sweetshop

"Mrs Floss," said Inspector Stilton, "we are investigating a robbery at the museum."

"What a coincidence," said Mrs Floss. "I think I've been robbed, too. I'm missing six red-and-yellow lollipops."

"Don't worry," said the inspector. "I can see them all here in this room."

"And I can see ten carrots," Nat added.

Ms Rotunda, Junk shop

"What excellent timing, Inspector," said Ms Rotunda. "I hope you can help me. All my clocks are either broken or wrong—except two. Which two are showing the right time?"

"Hmm," said Inspector Stilton, "two clocks showing the same time…"

"Aha!" said Nat. "There are ten elephants in this shop!"

Mr Rambutan, Fruit shop

"Good morning, Mr Rambutan," said Inspector Stilton. "We're here to investigate—"

"Ah, detective, thank goodness you're here. My last delivery of mangoes contained ten tropical fruit snails, and now they are loose in the shop! Please help me find them before they eat all my stock."

"Gladly," said the inspector.

"That's funny," said Nat. "I can't see any snails, but I can see ten fish."

Ms Swoon, Art gallery

"Ah, Inspector Stilton. How convenient. I recently purchased these seven paintings, as I was told they were the work of Otto Spotto (1853-1890), who always painted exactly from life. But now I suspect they may be fakes!"

Inspector Stilton studied the paintings carefully. "Yes," he said. "Unfortunately, they are all fakes. They were not painted by Otto Spotto—and there is a mistake in each one."

"I don't know much about art," admitted Nat, "but I can see ten pencils in this shop."

Mr Drillbit, Hardware shop

"Good morning, Mr Drillbit," said Inspector Stilton. "We're trying to track down a thief…"

"Hello, Inspector," Mr Drillbit replied. "I'm trying to track down the end of this reel of cord. I need a length of it for a customer—but what a tangle!"

"It's just like a maze," remarked the inspector. "And I happen to be very good at mazes."

"Apart from you and me, Inspector," Nat noted, "there are ten rats in this shop."

Monsieur Mousse, Cake shop

"Bonjour, detective," said the cake shop owner. "Perhaps you can help me. I have a very difficult customer. These are the things he doesn't like in a cake:
    an even number of layers,
    green fruit or yellow icing,
    pink cakes, unless there are cherries on top,
    two different kinds of fruit, or
    brown and orange cake together.
Do I have any cakes he will like?"

"You do," said Inspector Stilton. "But only one."

"Does he like banana cake?" asked Nat. "I can see ten bananas."

Ms Spangle, Costume shop

"Ms Spangle—" Inspector Stilton began.

"What do you think of this new hat, detective?" interrupted Ms Spangle. "I'm decorating it with these star-shaped buttons, but I need ten more. I'm sure they're here somewhere. Can you see them?"

"It's odd that there are ten rabbits," Nat remarked.

Miss Flora, Florist

"Hello, Inspector," said Miss Flora. "I could certainly use your help! I want to make up a bouquet using only one kind of flower, but in three different colours. Can you see a type of flower I could use?"

"Well, Miss Flora," said Inspector Stilton, "there is only one combination possible."

"Birds must like flowers," observed Nat. "I can see ten birds."

Mr Friz, Ice-cream parlour

"Ah, welcome," said Mr Friz. "You know, Inspector, I love ice-cream. Every day, I make myself a delicious sundae, with one scoop of ice-cream, some topping, and a little biscuit. Now, I have five flavours of ice-cream, four toppings and three kinds of biscuit. How many different sundaes can I make?"

"Let me see…" said Inspector Stilton.

"Maybe we need to taste all the sundaes,"
suggested Nat. "But Mr Friz, why are there ten seals
in your shop?"

Mrs Figg, Toyshop

"Good morning, Mrs Figg," said Inspector Stilton. "We—"

"Oh, Inspector!" interrupted Mrs Figg. "Someone raced through the shop and made me drop all these boxes. Now I have to put all the puzzles back together. But which are the two missing pieces of this jigsaw?"

"I'm sure I can help you," said Stilton. "I like puzzles."

"There are a lot of sheep in this shop," said Nat. "I can see ten."

Mr Angus, China shop

"You're just in time, Inspector," said Mr Angus. "Mrs Hopper wants to buy a present for a friend who doesn't like flowers, fruit, spots, stripes or anything red or green. Can you help me find something?"

"What a picky friend!" said Inspector Stilton. "Luckily, I can see three things that would be suitable."

"Inspector," called Nat. "Did you notice the ten turtles in this shop?"

"Well, we've recovered all the stolen treasures, Nat," Stilton said. "But the thief is still walking free in this very square. All that remains is to put him behind bars."

"How are we going to do that?" asked Nat. "We don't have any proof!"

"Oh yes we do," said Stilton wisely. "The thief left pieces of evidence behind in every shop. Did you see them?"

SEARCH • SEEK • SOLVE • SOLUTIONS

- The missing treasures (the thief hid one in each shop)
- The hidden shapes spotted by Nat (there are actually 11, not 10!)

The street

Mrs Floss, Sweetshop

Ms Rotunda, Junk Shop

Mr Rambutan, Fruit shop

Ms Swoon, Art gallery

Mr Drillbit, Hardware shop

Monsieur Mousse, Cake shop

Ms Spangle, Costume shop

Miss Flora, Florist

Mr Friz can make 60 different combinations of sundaes in his ice-cream parlour.

Mr Friz, Ice-cream parlour

Mrs Figg, Toyshop

Mr Angus, China shop

For Mum and Dad—JR

Little Hare Books
4/21 Mary Street, Surry Hills
NSW 2010 AUSTRALIA

First published in 2003
Reprinted in 2004

National Library of Australia
Cataloguing-in-Publication entry

Rossell, Judith.
I spy with inspector stilton.

For children.
ISBN 1 877003 29 8.

1. Picture puzzles - Juvenile literature. I. Title.
793.73

Designed and typeset by ANTART
Printed in China
Produced by Phoenix Offset

2 4 5 3

Twelve priceless objects have been stolen
from the museum!

It sounds like a job for Inspector Stilton
and his assistant, Nat—and YOU!

S E A R C H
for the missing treasure

S E E K
the clues the thief left behind

S O L V E
many more tricky puzzles along the way!

LITTLE HARE

ISBN 1-877003-29-8